By Gina Gold
Illustrated by Loter, Inc.

ABDOPUBLISHING.COM

Reinforced library bound edition published in 2016 by Spotlight, a division of ABDO
PO Box 398166, Minneapolis, Minnesota 55439. Spotlight produces high-quality reinforced library
bound editions for schools and libraries. Published by agreement with Disney Enterprises, Inc.

Printed in the United States of America, North Mankato, Minnesota.
042015   092015

 **DISNEP PRESS**
New York • Los Angeles

THIS BOOK CONTAINS
RECYCLED MATERIALS

LIBRARY OF CONGRESS CATALOGING-IN-PUBLICATION DATA

This title was previously cataloged with the following information:

Gold, Gina.
 Minnie : Hocus bow-cus / by Gina Gold ; illustrated by Loter, Inc.
  p. cm. (World of reading ; Level 1)
Summary: Minnie hires Penguini the Magnificent to put on a magic show at her fashion line release
party, but when Penguini leaves to get his lucky bow tie, Millie and Melody must jump in and save the
day.
1. Mouse, Minnie (Fictitious character)--Juvenile fiction. 2. Magic tricks--Juvenile fiction. 3. Humorous
stories. I. Loter, Inc., ill.
[E]--dc23
PZ7.G5624 Ho 2014
               2014936374

978-1-61479-363-2 (reinforced library bound edition)

Spotlight
A Division of ABDO
abdopublishing.com

Minnie's Bow-tique is having a magic show.

"Come see my new line of bows,"
says Minnie. "They are magical!"

Meet Penguini the magician!
Millie and Melody are his helpers.

Penguini fixes his cape.

"Oh, no!" he cries.

"I forgot my lucky bow tie."

"I cannot go on without it!"
he says. "I'll be back!"

Everyone waits and waits.

"What should we do?" asks Daisy.

Minnie has an idea.
Millie and Melody know
the tricks.
They can do the show!

"I know the card trick," says Millie.

"I know the bunny trick," says Melody.
"Let's do it!" the girls cry.

Millie has Clarabelle pick a card.
"Now put it back," she says.

"I'll say the magic words," says Millie.
"Presto change-o!"
Cuckoo-Loca has Clarabelle's card!

"Presto change-o!"
Millie has a scarf!

"Presto change-o!"
Melody has flowers!

"Presto change-o!"
Daisy has a coin.

"Don't you just love magic?"
Minnie says.

"Now for my last trick," Melody says.
"I will pull a bunny from this hat!"
She says the magic words.
"Presto change-o!"

Uh-oh. No bunny!

"We made everyone disappear!
Now we have to get them back,"
says Millie. "Hocus pocus!"
"Nope," says Melody.

Cuckoo-Loca tries to help.
"Abracadabra!" she says.

It works!
"But they are covered in bows!
We need Penguini!"
says Daisy.

"I am here!" says Penguini.
"We need your help," says Minnie.

"I said 'presto change-o,'" says Melody.

"I said 'hocus pocus,'" says Millie.

"I said 'abracadabra,'" says Cuckoo-Loca.

"But the magic words for this trick are . . . 'hocus bow-cus'!" says Penguini.

The bunny trick works!
Everything is okay.

"That is much better," says Minnie.

"We forgot the magic words,"
says Millie.
"We got all mixed up,"
says Melody.

"It's okay!" Minnie says.
"We all make mistakes."

"Minnie is right," says Penguini.
"It even happens to the great
Penguini."

"Look!" says Daisy.
"The Bow-tique is hopping!"

"But where is the bunny now?" says Minnie.

"Hocus bow-cus!" the twins cry.
"One bunny coming right up!"